Cesare Pavese was a novelist, poet, translator, editor, and literary critic, considered one of the most influential Italian intellectuals of the twentieth century. Born in 1908 in Santo Stefano Belbo, a small village in the Langhe region of Piedmont, he graduated from the University of Turin with a thesis on the poetry of Walt Whitman.

Pavese played a key role in introducing Italian readers to major English and American writers, translating works by authors such as Joyce, Defoe, Melville, and Faulkner. As an editor at the prestigious Einaudi publishing house, Pavese oversaw the publication of novels by Natalia Ginzburg and Italo Calvino.

A pioneer of literary neorealism, Pavese's work explores themes of loneliness and alienation, often featuring protagonists struggling to reconnect with a simpler rural past.

Pavese battled depression throughout his life. In 1950, two months after winning the Strega Prize, Italy's most prestigious literary award, and following a failed love affair with Hollywood actress Constance Dowling, he tragically ended his life in a hotel room near Turin's railway station.

Ben Sharafski is a writer and translator who lives in Sydney's Northern Beaches. His collection of interlinked short stories, *Returning to Carthage*, was recently published to critical acclaim.

CW01497140

Translated from the Italian *La spiaggia*
Published by Lewis & Greene
PO Box 70 Newport Beach NSW 2106

English translation © Ben Sharafski 2024
Edited by M. A. Hislop

ISBN 978-0-6450977-3-3 (Paperback)
ISBN 978-0-6450977-4-0 (eBook)

Cover illustration : Oleksii Arseniuk (iStock / Getty Images)
Book and cover design : Nohemy Adrian

A catalogue record for this work is available from the National Library of Australia

CESARE PAVESE

THE BEACH

a novella

Translated from the Italian by Ben Sharafski

Lewis & Greene

MODERN CLASSICS

1

FOR QUITE SOME time, my friend Doro and I had
agreed that I would be his guest. I was very fond of
Doro, and when he got married and moved to Genoa,
it almost made me sick. When I wrote to him to
decline the invitation to his wedding, I received a dry
and brash reply saying that if he couldn't use his
money to settle in the town his wife liked, then he
didn't know what he should use it for. Then one fine
day, passing through Genoa, I turned up at his house
and we made peace. I really liked his wife, a naughty
girl who charmingly asked me to call her Clelia and
left us alone just long enough, and when she reappeared in the evening to go out with us, she had
become such an enchanting lady that if I hadn't been
myself I would have kissed her hand.

I came to Genoa several times that year and always
went to see them. They were rarely alone, and Doro,
in his nonchalant way, seemed to fit in well with his

wife's circle. Or should I say rather that it was his wife's circle that had recognised him as their own man, and Doro let them be, carefree and in love. Every now and then he and Clelia would take the train and go on a trip, a kind of intermittent honeymoon that lasted almost a year. But they had enough tact to hardly mention it. Knowing Doro, I was glad of this silence, but also envious: Doro is one of those who are silenced by happiness, and when I saw him always calm and focused on Clelia, I understood how much he must be enjoying his new life. It was actually Clelia who, having gained some confidence in me, said to me one day when Doro had left us alone: "Oh yes, he is happy" — and she stared at me with a furtive and irrepressible smile.

They had a small villa on the Ligurian Riviera and often went there on their short trips. That was the villa where I was supposed to be their guest. But that first summer my work took me elsewhere, and I must say that I felt a certain embarrassment at the idea of intruding on their intimacy. Then again, seeing them, as I always did, in their Genoese circle, moving breathlessly from one trivial conversation to the next, enduring the rounds of their parties, which I found boring — ultimately it seemed that making a whole journey just to exchange a glance with him or a few words with Clelia was not worth the effort. I began to reduce my flying visits and turned into a letter-writer — sending greeting cards and the occasional gossip, replacing my old companionship with Doro as best I could. Sometimes it was Clelia who replied — a quick, flowing handwriting and charming updates, intelligently chosen from the shimmering jumble of thoughts and facts of another life and another world. I had the impression, however, that it was Doro himself who, out of lack of interest, had handed this task over to Clelia, and this saddened me, so that without any great flashes of jealousy, I distanced myself even further from them. I wrote perhaps three more times in a year, and one winter I had a fleeting visit from Doro, who didn't leave me alone for a single hour and spoke to me about his business — that's what he came for — but also about the old things that interested us both. He seemed more expansive than before, which wasn't surprising after such a long separation. He renewed his invitation to spend a holiday with them at the villa. I told him that I accepted, on the condition that I would live alone in a hotel and only be with them when we all felt like it. "All right," Doro said, laughing, "Do what you want. We won't eat you." Then I heard nothing for almost a year, and when the holiday season came, I happened to be free and without any plans. Then it was my turn to write and ask if they wanted to have me. I got a telegram from Doro: "Don't move. I'm coming."

2

WHEN I SAW him in front of me, summery and tanned, I almost didn't recognise him; my anxiety turned into spite.

"You can't treat people like that," I told him.

He laughed.

"Did you have a fight with Clelia?"

"Of course not! I have things to do," he said. "Keep me company."

We walked together all morning and even discussed politics. Doro was speaking in a strange way; I told him several times not to raise his voice. He had an aggressive and sardonic attitude that I hadn't seen in him for a long time. I tried to ask him about his affairs with the intention of bringing the conversation back to Clelia, but he immediately started laughing and said: "Leave my business alone. We don't really care about it, do we?" Then we walked a little farther in silence, and I began to feel hungry. I asked him if he wanted me to get him anything. "Might as well sit down," he said. "Do you have anything to do?"

"I was supposed to be going to see you."

"Then you can keep me company."

And he sat down first. The whites of his eyes sometimes darted around against his tan, restless as a dog's. Now that I had him in front of me, I realised that he appeared sardonic mainly due to the contrast between his teeth and his face. But he didn't give me the time to mention it, and said right away, "We haven't seen each other for ages."

I wanted to see where he was heading. I was annoyed. I even lit my pipe to show him that I had time on my side. Doro pulled out his gold-tipped cigarettes, lit one, and blew the smoke in my face. I remained silent, waiting.

But it was only when darkness fell that he let himself go. At noon, we ate together at a *trattoria*, drenched in sweat; then we resumed walking, and he entered several shops to show me that he had errands to run. Towards evening, we took the old hill road that we had often walked together in the old days, and ended up in a small lounge, something between a brothel and a trattoria that, back when we were students, had seemed to us the epitome of vice. We took a stroll under the cool summer moon, which offered some relief from the day's stifling heat.

"Do your relatives still live in the country?" I asked Doro.

"Yes, but I'm not going to visit them anyway. I want to be alone."

This, from Doro, was a compliment. I decided to make peace with him.

"Sorry," I said softly. "Can I come to the seaside with you?"

"Whenever you want," Doro said. "But first, keep me company. I want to escape to my old region."

We talked about it over dinner. We were served by one of the owner's daughters, a grubby and dishevelled girl, perhaps the same one who had often lured us there in the old days. But I saw that Doro paid no attention to her or to the younger sisters, who occasionally appeared to serve some couples in the corners. Doro drank, that's for sure, with great relish, and urged me to drink too, getting excited as he talked about his hills.

He had been thinking about them for a while, he told me; it had been — how long? — three years since he last saw them, and he needed a holiday. I listened, and the conversation ignited something within me as well. Many years before he got married, we had explored the entire region on foot with our backpacks, just the two of us, carefree and ready for anything, through the farms, near the villas, along the streams, sometimes sleeping in the barns. And the conversations we had — thinking about them now made me blush, or cringe in almost disbelief. We were at an age when we could listen to a friend's voice as if it were our own, when the two of us shared life in a way that I still believe — although I am a bachelor — married couples manage to experience.

"But why don't you go on the trip with Clelia?" I asked without malice.

"Clelia can't make it, she doesn't feel like it," Doro mumbled, putting down his glass. "I want to go with you." He said this emphatically, furrowing his brow and laughing, as he used to do during heated discussions.

"So, it's like being boys again," I grumbled, but maybe Doro didn't hear.

One thing I could not make clear that evening: whether Clelia knew about this getaway. Something in Doro's demeanour gave me the feeling that she didn't. But how could I again broach a topic that my friend was so stubbornly avoiding? That night, I had him sleep on my sofa; he had a rather restless sleep. I wondered why he waited until evening to tell me something as innocent as his plans for a trip. It irritated me to think that perhaps I was just a screen for an argument with Clelia. I have already mentioned that I have always been jealous of Doro.

This time we took the train early in the morning and arrived before it got too hot. At the far reaches of a landscape so immense it made the trees look tiny rose Doro's hills: dark, wooded hills that stretched their morning shadows over the yellow hillocks, scattered with farmhouses. Doro — I had resolved to keep an eye on him — now faced the trip with great calm. I had managed to get him to agree that it would last three days at most. I had also talked him out of bringing his suitcase.

We got off the train, looking around, and while Doro, who knew everyone, entered the Station Hotel, I stopped in the deserted square — so deserted that I looked at the clock, hoping it might be already noon. It wasn't nine yet, so I carefully studied the newly-laid cobblestones and the low houses with their green shutters and balconies blooming with wisteria and geraniums. The villa that had once belonged to Doro stood outside the village on the spur of a valley opening onto the plain. We had spent a night there during the famous trip, in an old room with lintels decorated with floral patterns, leaving in the morning with the beds unmade and without bothering to do anything but shut the gate behind us. I didn't have time to stroll through the grounds that surrounded it. Doro was born in that house — his parents lived there all year round and died there — and when he got married, he sold it. I was curious to see his face in front of that gate.

But when we left the hotel to take a walk, Doro went off in a completely different direction. We crossed the railway and went down along the river. It was obvious that he was looking for a shady spot, in the same way you'd look for a café in the city. "I thought we were going to the villa," I grumbled. "Wasn't that the whole point of coming here?"

Doro stopped, eyeing me. "What do you think? That I'm going back to my roots? What matters is in my blood, and nobody can take that away from me. I'm here to drink some of my wine and sing a little with people I know. I'm just going to have some fun."

I wanted to tell him, "That's not true," but I kept silent. I kicked a stone and took out my pipe. "You know I'm a terrible singer," I said through gritted teeth. Doro shrugged.

The morning and afternoon passed in peaceful wandering, through the ups and downs of the hillock. It seemed as if Doro was deliberately leading us down little paths that led nowhere, but at last ended in the sweltering heat on a dry riverbed, against a hedge, in front of a closed gate. Towards evening, when the sun, already low over the plain, filled it all with dust and the sweet acacias began to tremble in the breeze, we also went back up a stretch of the road that crossed the valley. I felt revived, and Doro became more talkative too. He spoke of a certain peasant who, in his day, was famous for kicking his sisters out of the house — he had quite a few — and then making the rounds of the farms where they had sought refuge, appearing to be beside himself and demanding a reconciliation lunch. "Who knows if he's still alive," Doro said. He used to live in a farmhouse that could be seen from there. He was a wiry little man who spoke little and was feared by all. But there was one thing he wouldn't do: he wouldn't get married because he said he would regret it if he had to throw his wife out too. One of the sisters had then really run away, causing general satisfaction in the village.

"What was he? A typical local?" I said.

"No, a man born for something else, a misfit, one of those who learn to be sly because they lead a life that doesn't satisfy them."

"Everyone should be sly, then."

"Indeed."

"Did he ever get married?"

"Of course not. He kept himself a sister, the sturdiest one, who bore him children and worked the vineyard. And they were fine. And perhaps they're still fine."

Doro spoke with a sarcastic tone, and as he spoke, he turned his eyes to the hill.

"Have you ever told this story to Clelia?"

Doro didn't answer; he seemed to be thinking of something else.

"Clelia is the type to enjoy hearing it," I continued, "Especially since it's not about your sister."

But all I got in response was a smile. Doro, when he wanted to, smiled like a boy. He stopped, placing his hand on my shoulder. "Have I ever told you that one year I brought Clelia here?" he said. Then I stopped too. I said nothing and waited.

Doro continued, "I thought I had told you. She asked me herself. We drove here with some friends. We were always driving around in those days."

He looked at me, and then at the hill behind me. He started to walk again and I moved with him.

"No, you haven't told me," I muttered. "When was that?"

"Not that long ago," Doro said. "Last year."

"And did she ask you to do it?"

Doro nodded.

"But you've wasted too much time," I said. "You should have brought her here earlier. Why did you leave her by the sea this year?"

But Doro was already smiling in that way of his. He gestured with his eyes towards the steep slope of the highest hill and did not answer. We climbed silently, while there was still light, and from the top we paused to look down into the plain, where we thought we could make out the dark clump of the forbidden villa in the dusty abyss.

As night fell, friendly faces began to appear in the hotel. There was a pool table, and people were playing. People around Doro's age — some office workers and a labourer covered in lime splashes — recognised him and made a big fuss over him. Then an elderly gentleman with a gold chain on his waistcoat came over and said he was delighted to meet me. While Doro played and joked around, the old man drank coffee with grappa and, leaning confidentially across the table, began to inquire about Doro's affairs. He told me the whole story of the villa, which had been bought by a certain Matteo when it was just a simple barn, with all the surrounding land. This Matteo was some kind of ancestor of Doro's, but then Doro's grandfather had started selling off the land in bits and pieces to build the house, and in the end all that was left was this big villa, without any land around it; and he had predicted to his friend, Doro's father, that one fine day his sons would sell the house too, leaving him like a tramp in the cemetery. He spoke a good-natured Italian flavoured with dialect; I don't know why, but I pictured him as a notary. Then some bottles arrived, and Doro drank standing, leaning on the pool cue, winking here and there. At some point, the only people remaining were the labourer, named Ginio, the two of us, and a big fellow in a red tie whom Doro hadn't met before. We left the hotel for a walk, the moon showing us the way. Under the moon, we all became like the labourer, whose face was covered with a mask of lime splashes. Doro spoke in his dialect; I understood it but couldn't respond fluently, and that made us laugh. The moon bathed everything, even the great hills, in a transparent vapour that veiled and erased every memory of the day. The fumes of the wine we had did the rest: I no longer bothered to wonder what Doro had in mind. I walked beside him, surprised and happy that we had rediscovered the secret of many years ago.

The labourer took us to his house. He told us to be quiet so as not to wake the women and his father. He left us in the farmyard in front of the big dark holes of the barn, in the strip of shadow of a haystack, and reappeared shortly afterwards, barefoot, with two black bottles under his arm, laughing like an idiot. We all sneaked down through the paddock behind the house, taking the dog with us, and sat down on the edge of a ditch. We had to drink straight from the bottle, which the fellow with the tie didn't like, but Ginio said, laughing, "If you can't do it, you're a loser," and we all drank.

"We can sing here," Ginio said, clearing his throat. He began to sing on his own, and his voice filled the valley; the dog wouldn't keep quiet any longer; other dogs answered from near and far, and then ours began to bark. Doro laughed loudly, his voice filled with happiness, then took another gulp and joined in Ginio's song. Together they quickly silenced the dogs, at least enough for me to realise that the song was melancholy, lingering on the lowest notes, with strangely gentle words in that rough dialect. Of course, it could be that the moon and the wine have contributed to the way I remember them. What I'm sure of is the joy, the sudden bliss I felt when I reached out my hand to touch Doro's shoulder. I felt a gasp in my breath, and suddenly I loved him, because after so long we were together again.

That other fellow, named Biagio, would occasionally bellow a note or a phrase, then lower his head again and resume his interrupted conversation with me. I explained that I didn't live in Genoa, and that I had a government job thanks to an old degree I had taken when I was young.

Then he told me he wanted to get married, but he wanted to do it right, and to do something right you had to be as lucky as Doro, who had found a wife and a business in Genoa at the same time. The word 'business' made me angry, and I lost my patience and said abruptly: "But do you know Doro's wife? If you don't, just shut up."

It's when I treat people like this that I realise I'm over thirty. I thought about it for a while that night, as Doro and the labourer began to reminisce about their time in the regiment. The bottle came to me — before passing it, white-faced Ginio had wiped it with the palm of his hand — and I took a long gulp, trying to release in the wine the feelings I couldn't express in song.

"Yes sir, excuse me," said Ginio, taking back the bottle, "but if you come back next year, I'll be married and I'll open one for you at my place."

"Do you always let your father boss you around?" Doro asked.

"It's not that I let him, he just does it."

"He's been bossing you around for thirty years. Hasn't your back given out yet?"

"It would be easier for you to break his," the fellow with the tie said, laughing nervously.

"And what does he say about Orsolina? Will he let you marry her?"

"We don't know yet," Ginio said, pulling his legs out of the ditch and suddenly wriggling across the grass like an eel. "If he doesn't let me, all the better," he muttered, a couple of steps away. Every time I see the moon I remember that little fellow, white as a baker, who was always fooling around and addressed Doro with the familiar *tu*. Later, I made Clelia burst out laughing when I described him to her. She laughed with that contented look of hers and said, "Doro is such a child. He'll never change."

But I didn't tell Clelia what happened next. Ginio and Doro launched into another song, and this time all four of us joined in, singing out of tune. It came to an end when a furious voice from the farmhouse yelled at us to stop. In the sudden silence, Biagio shouted something rude and defiantly resumed the song. Doro was also starting again when Ginio jumped to his feet. "No," he stammered. "He recognised me. It's my father." But that Biagio wasn't having any of it; Ginio and Doro had to jump on him to shut him up. Staggering and slipping on the grass, we had barely moved away when Doro had an idea. "The Murette sisters," he said to Ginio. "We can't sing here, but they used to sing in the old days. Let's go to Rosa's." And off he went right away, but the young man took my arm and whispered to me in dismay: "This means trouble. The sergeant lives there." I wasn't sure what to do, but I caught up with Doro and struggled to hold onto the thick muscle of his arm. "Don't mix wine and women, Doro," I shouted at him in agitation. "Remember, we are gentlemen."

Nevertheless, Ginio came on determined and admitted that those three girls had put on weight, but we weren't going there for that, just to sing a little. Even if they were fat, what did it matter? A woman must be solidly built. He struggled and pulled Doro and said: "You'll see that Rosa will remember." We were now on the main road, under the moonlight, all worked up and huddled around Doro, who was strangely indecisive.

Rosa had won, because the young man said angrily: "Don't you understand that they don't want you because you're dirty with lime?" And he took a punch in the face which made him move back three steps and spit on the ground. Then he vanished as if by magic, and for a moment we heard him shout in the silence of the moon: "Thank you, *Ingeniere*. I'm going to tell Ginio's father!"

Doro and Ginio were already on their way, and I followed. I didn't know what to say, because I too was wavering. If I had any misgivings, it was only that this dirty labourer was outdoing me in front of Doro in terms of the intensity of their shared memories, which they recalled animatedly as they walked towards the village. They spoke at random, and the thick dialect was enough to give Doro back the authentic flavour of his life, of the wine, the flesh, and the happiness in which he was born. I felt like an intruder, inept. I took Doro's arm and thrust myself forward, grunting. After all, I had the same wine in my body.

What we did under those windows was reckless. I figured out that Biagio must have been lying in wait in some corner of the square, and I told that to Doro, who wasn't even listening. First Ginio, laughing like an idiot, knocked on the worm-eaten little door, under the moon. We spoke in whispers, amused and excited. But no one answered, and the windows remained closed. Then Doro started coughing, and Ginio began to gather stones and throw them up. Then we argued, because I said he was going to break the glass, and finally Doro unleashed himself with a terrible, beastly scream, modulated like those that country drunkards make after one of their choruses. It seemed to make all the silences of the moon tremble. Various distant dogs, from some unknown courtyards, responded to us furiously.

Doors slammed and shutters creaked. Ginio also started singing out of tune, something reminiscent of his earlier song, but Doro's voice quickly caught up with his and drowned it out. Someone shouted at the other side of the square, a light flashed in the window; we fell silent. We had just heard the litany of curses and threats start when the labourer threw himself at the small door, battering it with kicks and punches. Doro grabbed my shoulder and pulled me into the strip of shadow of the house next door. "Let's see if they pour the basin over him," he whispered hoarsely, laughing, "I want to see him soaked like a goose."

A dog barked very close by; I started to feel ashamed of myself. We then fell silent again: even Ginio, who was clutching a bare foot in his hands and hopping on the cobblestones. As we grew quiet, the voices from the windows also faded away; the light disappeared; only the intermittent barking persisted. It was then that we heard the cautious creaking of the shutter above.

Ginio slumped into the shade between us. "They've opened it," he muttered in our faces. I pushed him away, remembering that he was all covered in lime. "Go on, let them know it's you," Doro said dryly. Ginio called out from the darkness, looking up. I felt his cold, rough neck under my hand. "Let's sing," he said to Doro. Doro paid him no attention and whistled softly, as if calling a dog. Voices were chattering upstairs.

"Go on," said Doro, "let them know it's you," and he gave him a shove that sent him into the moonlight.

Ginio emerged into the light, staggering, still laughing, and raised his elbow as if to shield himself from an imaginary thrown object. All was silent at the window. His sagging trousers tripped him up, almost toppling him. He stumbled and sat down on the ground.

"Rosina, oh Rosina," he cried, his mouth gaping, but stifling his voice. "Do you know who's here?" There was a muffled laugh from above, which stopped immediately.

Ginio resumed his eel-like movements, this time on the hard ground. Placing his hands behind himself, he spun around, bringing himself back to the line of shade. Doro was already on his feet, ready to give him a kick. But Ginio was quick to jump up, shouting as he jumped, "It's Doro, Doro from Ca' Rosse, who's come from Genoa to see you all." He looked like a madman.

There was movement above and creaking and flashing glass; then a heavy thud against the door, which opened, splitting the white moonlight that flooded it. Ginio, nailed halfway through his dance, was only a few steps away from the threshold. A stocky man in shirtsleeves had appeared.

At that moment a sharp, insolent voice came from the other side of the square — Biagio's voice — shouting: "Marina, don't open, they're as drunk as animals." There were shouts from the window, heavy footsteps; I vaguely glimpsed flailing arms.

But already at the doorstep the man and Ginio had grabbed each other and were wrestling, groaning, shifting, panting like angry dogs. The man was wearing black trousers striped with red. Doro, who had been holding my shoulder, suddenly broke away and jumped into the fray. He threw a few random kicks, circling around, trying to join the melee. Then he broke away and stood under the window. "Are you Rosina or Marina?" he said, looking up. There was no answer. "Are you Rosina or Marina?" he shouted, with his foot on the threshold.

There followed a crash, something had fallen: as it turned out later it was a flower vase. Doro jumped back, still looking up, where at least two women were now moving excitedly.

"We didn't do it on purpose," said a woman's voice, harsh and commanding. "Did it hurt you?"

"Who's speaking?" Doro shouted. "I'm Marina," a softer, pleading voice said. "Have you been hurt?"

It was then that I stepped out of the shadows to have my say. Ginio and the other man had separated and were circling each other, swinging their arms angrily and grunting. But suddenly the *carabiniere* jumped back to the door in two leaps, pulling Doro away and throwing him back. The women upstairs screamed.

All around the square windows began to fly open again, and irritated, angry voices crossed each other. The man had closed the door, and we heard the wooden bar slam into place. Above our heads crossed a barrage of insults and complaints, dominated by the harsh voice of the first of the two women. I heard — and this is what finally sobered me from the wine — Doro's name being passed from window to window. Ginio had another go at the door, hitting it and shouting. From the windows across the square, apples and certain hard projectiles — peach stones — began to rain down on us, and then, just as Doro grabbed Ginio and was pulling him away, there was a flash from the window and a loud explosion that silenced everyone.

3

THE FIRST EVENING, when we went for a walk by the sea together, I told Clelia as much as I could about Doro's adventure — which was next to nothing. Still, the extravagance of it made her smile sullenly. "How selfish of you," she said. "I was bored here. Why didn't you take me with you?"

When she saw us arrive the afternoon after our escapade, Clelia showed no sign of surprise. I hadn't seen her for more than two years. We met her on the steps of the villa, dressed in shorts, chestnut-haired and tanned. She held out her hand to me with a confident smile. Her eyes kept moving, sharper and harder than they used to be, standing out against her tan. She immediately started talking about what we were going to do the next day. She had delayed going down to the beach so she could welcome me. I jokingly told her that Doro was exhausted and left them alone to catch up.

That first evening, I went looking for a room, and I found one in a secluded alley, with a window overlooking a large, contorted olive tree, inexplicably grown right in the middle of the cobblestones. Many times after that, when I returned to my room alone, I happened to look at it, lost in thought, and that is perhaps the most vivid memory I have of the whole summer. Seen from below, it was gnarled and bare; but when I leaned out from my room's window it was a solid silvery mass of curled dry leaves. It gave me the feeling of being in the country, in an unknown countryside, and I often sniffed thinking it might smell of sea salt. I have always found it strange that on the very edge of the coast, between land and sea, plants and flowers grow and good drinking water flows. My room was reached by an external stone staircase, which was steep and angular. While I shaved and cleaned up, I could sometimes hear from the ground floor below me a din of discordant voices. Some of them were women's; I couldn't tell if they were happy or angry. As I walked down the stairs, I looked in through the bars of the windows, but the twilight had darkened the rooms. It was only after I had moved away that one voice dominated the others, like someone singing a solo, a fresh and strong voice that I couldn't name but that I had heard before. I was about to turn back to unravel the mystery when it occurred to me that we were neighbours after all, and that getting to know your neighbours always happens too soon.

"Doro is in the forest," Clelia said that evening as we walked along the beach. "He's painting the sea." She turned as she walked and glanced around. "The sea deserves to be painted. You should look at it too."

We looked at the sea, and then I told her that I didn't understand why she was bored. Clelia said, laughing, "Tell me again about the little man in the moonlight. What was he shouting about? I was also looking at the moon the other night."

"He was probably making faces. Four drunks aren't enough to make you laugh."

"Were you drunk?"

"Obviously."

"You're such boys," Clelia said.

Between us, Ginio's night became a running joke, and all I had to do was allude to the little white man and his antics for Clelia to light up with joy. But when I told her that evening that Ginio wasn't a bald old man, but someone of Doro's age, she grimaced in dismay. "Why did you tell me that? You've ruined everything. Was he a peasant?"

"A bricklayer, to be exact."

Clelia sighed.

"After all," I said, "you've seen the village too. You can imagine what it's like. If Doro had been born two doors down, you might have been Ginio's wife by now."

"How awful," Clelia said, smiling.

That night, after dinner on the balcony, while Doro sat stretched out in his chair, smoking in silence, and Clelia had gone to dress for the evening, I couldn't get the conversation we had a little earlier out of my head. They were talking about a certain Guido, a forty-year-old colleague of Doro's and a bachelor, whom I had already met in Genoa and then met again on the beach with Clelia's group — he was one of her friends. It turned out that it was with him that they had passed through Doro's village on that car trip. Clelia, enlivened by a sudden mischievous memory, told the whole story of that trip without any prompting, and as she spoke, she had the air of answering a question I hadn't asked. They were returning from some mountain expedition; their friend Guido was at the wheel, and Doro had said, "Do you know that I was born in these hills thirty years ago?" And then everyone, especially Clelia, had pestered Guido so much that he had agreed to take a detour up there. It was madness, because they had to tell the car behind them about the delay, and it took forever to arrive, so they waited for it at the fork for over an hour. When it finally arrived, it was getting dark, so after eating as best they could in the village, they had to climb mysterious little roads with no signs and cross so many hills that it was almost dawn when they found themselves back on the road to Genoa. Doro had sat down next to Guido to help him with the directions, and no one had been able get any sleep. A real madness.

Now that Clelia wasn't there, I asked Doro if they had made up. As I spoke, I thought, "What they need is a child," but it was a subject I had never broached with Doro, except in jest. And Doro said, "Peace is made by those who have made war. What war have you ever seen me make?" I immediately fell silent. Despite our closeness, the subject of Clelia had never been discussed between us. I was about to tell him that you could make war by jumping on a train and running away, for example, but I hesitated and then Clelia called me.

"What mood is Doro in?" she asked through the room's closed door.

"Good," I stammered, without coming in.

"Are you sure?"

Clelia came to the door, fixing her hair. Her eyes searched for me in the semi-darkness where I was waiting for her.

"You two are friends, and you don't know that when Doro lets himself be teased without reacting, it means he's annoyed and irritated?"

So I tried it with her. "Haven't you two made up yet?"

Clelia withdrew to her room and fell silent. Then she reappeared, ready to go, saying, "Why don't you turn on the light?" She took my arm and we walked across the dimly lit room. As we were about to step out onto the illuminated landing, Clelia tightened her grip on my arm and whispered, "I'm desperate. I want Doro to spend a lot of time with you, because you're his friend. I know you do him good and take his mind off things..."

I tried to stop and speak.

"No, we haven't had a fight," Clelia said quickly. "And he's not jealous. And he doesn't want to hurt me. It's just that he's become a different person. We can't reconcile because we never fought. Do you understand? But don't say anything."

That night, as usual, we ended up in Guido's car, and drove along the winding road, bustling with beachgoers, to a nightclub high above the sea. A small band was playing and some people were dancing. But the attraction of the place lay in the tables with shaded lamps scattered in rocky nooks on the cliff overlooking the sea. The scent of aromatic and flowering plants mixed with the sea breeze, and you could glimpse the rows of tiny lights jutting out along the coast below.

I tried to be alone with Clelia, but I didn't get a chance. One moment, I found Doro next to me, then Guido, then one of her female friends — they came and went one after the other. However, because they kept changing dance partners, it was impossible to start a conversation, and Clelia was always busy. At some point I said to her, "I'll dance too," to her delighted surprise, and I led her under the pine trees outside the fenced area. "Let's sit down," I said, "and you can tell me the whole story."

I tried to ask her why she hadn't confronted Doro. You have to provoke a crisis, I told her, like when you shake a watch to make it tick again. I refused to believe that a woman like her could not, with a simple tone of voice, force openness from a man who was still, after all, behaving like a boy.

"But Doro is open with me," Clelia said. "He even told me about the serenade you sang for Rosina. Did you have fun?"

I think I blushed, more out of annoyance than embarrassment.

"And I'm open too," Clelia continued, smiling. Her voice was sulky: "My friend Guido even says that my weakness is that I am open with everyone, that I do not give anyone the illusion that they have a secret all to themselves. People are so sweet! But that's the way I am. And that's why I fell in love with Doro..."

She paused and glanced at me. "Do you think I'm indecent?"

I didn't say anything. I was annoyed. Clelia fell silent, then continued. "You see, I'm right. But I am indecent. Just like Doro. That's why we love each other."

"So, let's make peace," I said. "What's all this fuss about?"

Here Clelia whimpered in that childish way of hers. "You see, you're just like the others. But don't you understand that we can't fight? We love each other. If I could hate him like I hate myself, then yes, I would abuse him. But neither of us deserves it. Do you understand?"

"No."

Clelia fell silent, and we listened to the gravel crunching and the band breaking up, and then someone starting to sing.

"What advice did your Guido give you?" I asked, in the same tone as before.

Clelia shrugged. "Self-serving advice. He's been trying to woo me."

"...to keep a secret from Doro?"

"To make him jealous," Clelia said ruefully. "That fool. He doesn't understand that Doro would let me do it and suffer in silence."

At this point, a friend from the group came looking for Clelia, called her and laughed. I was left alone, sitting on the bench. I felt my usual bitter pleasure in remaining apart, knowing that just a few steps away, outside the shadows, others were bustling about, laughing and dancing. And I had a lot to think about. I lit a pipe and smoked it all out. Then I moved and wandered between the tables until I met Doro.

"How about a drink at the bar?" I said to him.

When we were alone, I began: "Just to get things straight, can I tell your wife that we had to run away the next morning to avoid being beaten up?"

We both just laughed. Then Doro replied with a half-smirk, "Did she ask you?"

"No. I'm asking you."

"Sure, tell her whatever you want."

"But aren't you two on bad terms?"

Doro raised his glass and stared at me absorbed in his thoughts. "No," he said calmly.

"Then why does Clelia sometimes look at you with frightened eyes, like a dog? She has the look of a beaten woman. Have you beaten her?"

At that moment, Clelia, who was twirling on the dance floor with some guy, shouted at us "Drunks!" and we saw her hand waving at us. Doro followed her with his eyes, nodding to her, lost in thought, until she disappeared behind the dancer's back.

"As you can see, she's happy," he said quietly. "Why should I beat her? We get on better than most. She's never said a bad word to me. We even agree on our entertainment, which is the biggest problem."

"I know you get along." I stopped myself.

Doro said nothing. He looked down at his glass, looking crestfallen, then lowered his head, held the glass at arm's length and emptied it quickly, half turning away, like someone clearing their throat in company.

"The trouble," he said in a concluding tone as he walked away, "is that we're too close to each other. You say certain things just to please the other person." Clelia and Guido approached us from between the tables.

"Are you speaking about me?" I said.

"About you too," Doro muttered.

4

WHEN I CAME to the seaside, I dreaded the thought of having to spend days swarming with strangers — shaking hands, saying thanks, and engaging in Sisyphean conversations. However, apart from the inevitable evenings with their friends, Clelia and Doro lived with a certain calm. Every evening, I dined with them at the villa, and their friends wouldn't arrive until after dark. Our trio was not lacking in warmth, and although all three of us had troubled thoughts to hide, we had many open-hearted conversations.

It was not long before I had a few adventures of my own to share: gossip from the trattoria where I had breakfast, bizarre thoughts, and strange incidents — the kind that the chaos of life by the sea tends to encourage. The next day I found out whose voice I had heard through the bars of the window that first evening as I came down the stairs. A sunburnt youth approached me on the beach, greeted me politely with a wave of his hand and then walked away. I only recognised him after he had gone by. He was just one of my students from the previous year who, one fine day, without warning, missed his usual lesson in my study — and I never saw him again. That same morning, as I was sunbathing, a dark and energetic body collapsed beside me — it was him again. He smiled, exposing his teeth, and asked me if I was going for a swim. I responded without lifting my head. I happened to be far from my friends' beach umbrella, and I had hoped to be alone. He straightforwardly explained that he had come to that beach by pure chance and was enjoying himself. He didn't say anything about the lesson business. Out of spite, I told him that I had heard his parents arguing the night before. He smiled again and replied that it was impossible, because his parents weren't there. But he admitted that he lived in a street with an olive tree in it. And as he got up to leave, he spoke of friends who were waiting for him. That evening, I poked my head into the ground floor, where there was an overpowering smell of frying, and I saw children, a woman in a headscarf, an unmade bed and stoves. As they had noticed me, I asked about him, and the woman — my own landlady — came to the door and, chatting away, thanked heaven that I knew her tenant, for she was already regretting taking him in, and wanted to write to his family — such good people, to send their son to the seaside to enjoy himself, and yet only the night before he had brought a woman to his room. "These things..." she said. "He's not eighteen yet."

I told Clelia and Doro the story, describing the visit that Berti paid me the next morning when he came to the top of the stairs, held out his hand and said, "Now that you know where I live, we'd better be friends."

"You'll see, the next thing he'll ask you to let him use your room," Doro said.

Encouraged by Clelia's attention, I continued. I explained that Berti's impertinence was merely shyness turned aggressive in self-defence. I said that the year before — before he'd disappeared and probably squandered the money he should have spent on my lessons — the boy had shown signs of submissiveness and used to bow awkwardly whenever he saw me. It was what always happens: reality disguises itself as its opposite. Like tender souls pretending to be rough. I envied him, I said, because, being so young, he could still deceive himself about his true nature.

"I think," Clelia said, "that I should have a closed, suspicious, and perverse character."

Doro smiled, saying nothing. "Doro doesn't believe it," I said, "but when he's being rough it's because he feels like crying."

The maid who was changing our plates stopped to listen. She blushed and hurried away; I continued. "Even as a boy he was like that. I remember him. He was one of those people who get offended when you ask them how they feel."

"If this were all true it would be easy to understand people," Clelia said.

These discussions would end when the others arrived after dinner. There was the usual Guido, who only left his car to play cards, a few ladies, some girls, the occasional husband — in short, the Genoese circle. It was nothing new to me that more than three people make a crowd, and that nothing worthwhile could be said then. I almost preferred the nights when we took the car and drove up the coast in search of cool air. Sometimes, in some scenic nightspot, while everyone was dancing, I could exchange a few words with Doro or Clelia, or talk utter nonsense with one of the ladies. A drink and the sea breeze were then all I needed to get myself on my feet again.

During the day, on the beach, it was a different story. People speak with a strange caution when they are half naked: words no longer sound the same. Sometimes, when they are silent, it seems that the silence itself gives rise to ambiguous words. Clelia had an ecstatic way of enjoying the sun as she lay on the rock, merging with it and flattening her body against the sky. She responded to the odd words of those beside her only with a whisper, a sigh, or a twitch of her knee or elbow. I soon realised that, lying there like that, Clelia wasn't really listening to anything. Doro, knowing this, never spoke to her. He sat on his towel, clasping his knees, gloomy and restless. He didn't lie down like Clelia; if he ever tried, after a few minutes he would twist, turn on his stomach, or sit up again.

But we were never alone. The whole beach swarmed and clamoured — that's why Clelia preferred the rocks, the hard and slippery stone, to everyone else's sand. Whenever she stood up, she would shake her hair, dazed and smiling, and ask us what we were talking about, looking around to see who was there. Her girlfriends were there, Guido was there, the whole group was there. Someone would come out of the water. Someone else would gingerly get in. Guido, in his white terrycloth robe, would arrive with new acquaintances whom he would dismiss at the foot of the beach umbrella. And then he would climb onto the rock and tease Clelia, never going into the water.

The best time was after midday or at sunset, when the warmth or the colour of the water persuaded even the most reluctant to go for a swim or a walk on the beach. Then we were nearly alone, with only that pleasant-talking Guido for company. Doro, who sought distraction from his melancholy in his brushes, would sometimes set up an easel on the rock

and paint boats, umbrellas, splashes of colour —
content to watch us from above and listen to our
chatter. Occasionally someone from the group would
arrive by boat, approach cautiously and call out to us.
In the silence that followed, we would listen to the
waves rippling between the rocks.

Our friend Guido used to say that this sound was
Clelia's weakness, her secret, her betrayal of all of us.

"I don't think so," Clelia said, "I listen to it naked,
stretched out in the sun, and anyone who wants to
can see me."

"Who knows," Guido said. "Who knows what
conversations a woman like you has with the waves. I
can imagine what you say to each other beforehand,
when you're in each other's arms."

Doro's seascapes — he made two of them in those
days — were painted in pale and indistinct colours, as
if the very intensity of the sun and the air, over-
whelming and blinding, had dulled his brushstrokes.
Someone climbed up behind Doro, followed his
hand and offered him advice. Doro did not answer.
Once he told me that you had to entertain yourself as
best you could. I tried to tell him not to paint from
life, because the sea was always more beautiful than
his paintings; all you had to do was look at it. In his
place, with his ability, I would have painted portraits;
it's satisfying to figure people out. Doro laughed and
replied that when the season was over, he would close
his paintbox and not think about it anymore.

One evening, while walking with Doro to the café where we were having our aperitifs, we joked about it. Our friend Guido remarked in his sly tone that no one would have guessed that beneath Doro's tough and dynamic man-of-the-world exterior slumbered the soul of an artist. "It slumbers all right," replied Doro, carefree and happy. "What doesn't slumber beneath the surface of all of us? You should have the courage to wake up and find yourself. Or at least talk about it. We don't talk enough about things in this world."

"Spill it out," I said to him. "What have you found out?"

"I haven't found out anything. But do you remember how much we used to talk when we were boys? We spoke just for the sake of talking. We knew very well they were just words, and yet we enjoyed it."

"Doro, Doro," I said to him, "you're getting old. Leave these things to those children you don't have."

At that, Guido started to laugh, a hearty laughter that made his eyes small. He put his hand around Doro's shoulder, supporting himself as he laughed. We looked incredulously at his balding head and the hard eyes of a handsome man on holiday.

"Something slumbers even in Guido," Doro said. "He sometimes laughs like an idiot."

Later I noticed that Guido only laughed like that among men. That evening, after dropping off Doro and Clelia at the gate of the villa, we left the car at the hotel and went for a stroll together, along the shore. We talked about our friends, almost without wanting to. Guido explained Doro's trip and his unexpected return by bringing up the restless artist. It was curious how Doro had managed to convince them all of the seriousness of his game. There was even talk in our group about encouraging him to exhibit his work and pursue art as a profession. "But of course, that's what I always tell him," Clelia would interject chattily.

"Crazy stuff," Guido said that evening.

"But Doro is joking," I said.

Guido was silent for a few steps — he was wearing sandals and we were advancing slowly, like a pair of monks — then he stopped and declared abruptly: "I know these two. I know what they're doing and what they want. But I don't know why Doro paints pictures."

"What's wrong with it? It distracts him."

The problem was that Doro, like all artists, did not satisfy his wife.

"What do you mean?"

"I mean that nervous brainwork weakens male potency, which is why every painter goes through periods of terrible depression."

"But not sculptors?"

"All of them," Guido grumbled, "all the madmen who strain their brains and don't know when it's time to stop."

We stopped outside the hotel. I asked him what kind of life he thought we should lead. "A healthy life," he said. "Work, but without overexerting yourself. Have fun, eat and talk. Above all, have fun."

He stood in front of me, rocking on his feet, with his hands behind his back. The open lapels of his shirt, exposing his chest, gave him the devious air of a know-it-all teenager, of a forty-year-old who's remained a teenager out of laziness. "You have to understand life," he said again, narrowing his eyes with an expression of unease. "Understand it while you're young."

5

CLELIA HAD TOLD me that every morning, Doro would run off to swim in the milky sea of dawn. That's why he would lazily linger behind his easel until midday. Sometimes, she said, she would join him, but not tomorrow, as she was too sleepy. I'd promised Doro I would keep him company, but I couldn't sleep that night. I got up at first light and walked through the cool, deserted streets to the still-damp beach. It was time to stop and watch the golden sunlight illuminate and outline the small trees on the mountaintop. But as I sat on the beach, I saw a head approaching in the still water, and the dark, dripping body of my young friend emerged.

Of course, he came up to talk to me, while rubbing his thin and short body with his towel. I looked out to sea to see if I could make out Doro's head.

"How come you're alone?" I asked.

He didn't answer — he was completely absorbed in his actions — and when he finished, he sat down a few steps away, facing the sea. I turned to the side to look at the mountain teeming with gold. Berti fumbled in a bundle with his fingertips, pulled out a cigarette and lit it. Then he apologised, saying that he only had one left.

I was surprised that he was such an early riser. Berti made a vague gesture and asked if I was expecting anyone. I told him that you don't wait for people on the beach. Then, with a sudden movement, Berti lay down on his stomach and, propped up on his elbows, smoked while looking at me.

He said he was disgusted by the festive atmosphere the beach took on in the sun. Children, umbrellas, nannies, families. If he had his way, he would ban them. So I asked him why he had come to the seaside: he could stay in the city, where there were no beach umbrellas.

"The sun will be up soon," he said, twisting his body to look at the mountain.

We were quiet for a while, in the barely rustling silence.

"Are you staying here long?" he asked me. I told him I didn't know and looked out to sea again. I could see a black spot. Berti also looked at it and said: "That's your friend. He was on the buoy when I arrived. He swims so well! Do you swim?"

After a while, he threw away his cigarette and stood up. "Are you home today?" he asked. "I need to talk to you."

"You can talk to me now," I said, looking up.

"But you're expecting people."

I told him not to be silly. What was it? Lessons?

Then Berti sat down again and stared at his knees. He began to talk like someone being interrogated, at times stopping for no apparent reason. The gist of it was that he was bored, had no company, and that he would be very, very happy to discuss things with me, to read some books together — no, not lessons — but to read as I used to at school, explaining and discussing, teaching them many things he knew he didn't know.

I gave him a look, reluctant but curious. Berti was one of those boys who come to school because they're sent there, and when you talk, they stare at your mouth with puffy, annoyed eyes. Now, naked and tanned, he hugged his knees and smiled restlessly. Who knows, I thought, maybe these boys are the most alert.

He left just as Doro's head was about to reach the shore. He stood up abruptly and said goodbye. Other bathers began to walk between the cabins, and it seemed to me that he was running after a skirt that disappeared behind one of them. But here was Doro coming out of the water, bent over as if climbing a mountain, smooth and dripping, with his head glistening under a cap that made him look very athletic. He stopped in front of me, swaying and panting; he still had the spasms of swimming under his breastbone and ribs. I couldn't help thinking of Guido and our conversation the night before, and a vague smile escaped me. Doro, pulling off his cap, grumbled: "What's the matter?"

"Nothing," I replied. "I've been thinking about that handsome guy Guido who's been putting on weight. Not getting married is really good for you!"

"If he swam for an hour every morning, he would look completely different," said Doro, falling to his knees on the sand.

Berti came looking for me in the trattoria at midday. He stopped between the tables with his jacket thrown over his dark blue singlet. I motioned for him to come over. He came, grabbing a chair from one of the tables, but the way I looked at him must have made him uncomfortable, because he stopped and his jacket slipped off his shoulders. Then he picked it up and let go of the chair. I told him to take a seat.

This time he offered me a cigarette, and immediately began to talk. I lit my pipe without answering. I just let him say what he had in mind. He told me that he'd had to give up his studies for family reasons, but that he hadn't found a job yet — and now that he'd given up, seeing me made him understand that studying was a smart thing to do, not as a student, but independently, for his own pleasure. He said he envied me and that he'd realised for some time that I was not only a teacher but also a nice person. He had many things he wanted to discuss with me.

"For example?" I said.

"For example," he replied, "why can't you learn by talking things over with the teacher, maybe even going for a walk with him? Was it really necessary to waste your time waiting for the four idiots who are holding up the whole class?"

"In fact, you were so eager to learn that school wasn't enough for you, and you took private lessons."

Berti smiled and said that that was a different matter.

"And I'm sorry," I continued, "to find out now that your parents aren't millionaires. Why did you make them spend money on private lessons?"

He smiled again, in a way that was both feminine and disdainful. Women react like that. A woman must have taught him that, I thought.

Berti accompanied me for a while — I was going on an outing with Clelia's friends that day — and told me once again that he understood very well that I had come to the seaside to relax and that he didn't think he had the right to force me to give him lessons, but at least, he hoped, I would tolerate his company and talk to him sometimes on the beach. This time it was I who gave him the girlish smile and, leaving him in the middle of the road, said: "Sure, if you really are alone."

The trip that day — we were all there, in Guido's car — had an unfortunate ending when one of the women, a certain Mara, a relative of Guido's, slipped off an overhanging rock while picking blackberries and injured her shoulder. We had climbed up the usual mountain road, past the nightclub, past the last scattered villas, through the pine trees and the red cliffs to the plateau where I had caught the first rays of sunlight that morning. Once we had carried the poor girl up to the road, it was clear that we wouldn't all fit in the car. Guido, who was very concerned, wanted to lay Mara, who was moaning, on the cushions. There was room left for Clelia and two other girls, who looked at me and Doro with amusement, and the two of us ended up walking back. After a couple of hundred steps, we spotted the second of the girls sitting on a pile of gravel.

Doro hastily concluded his remarks: "That's what it's like, being always surrounded by women."

This girl had been taken down to make room for Mara, who was moaning so much that she must have really broken her collarbone. It fell on her because she was the only unmarried girl in the group. "We're not women," she said, annoyed. "Mara's done having fun this year. They're taking her back to Genoa." As she walked, she glanced sideways at us. Doro gave her a small, friendly smile. They talked briefly about Mara and debated how her husband, that energetic man who only escaped from his office in Sestri on Sundays, would take it. "He'll be happy that it was his wife who's broken a bone," Doro said. "She'll finally be spending a summer with him."

The girl — her name was Ginetta — laughed sarcastically. "You think so?" she said, fixing her grey eyes on him. "I know that men like it when their wives are away. They're selfish."

Doro burst out laughing. "Such wisdom, Ginetta. I bet Mara isn't thinking about that right now." Then he looked at me. "It takes boys or bachelors to say such things."

"I'm not saying anything," I muttered.

This Ginetta was a good-looking girl who walked with energy and had the habit of tossing her hair back like a mane. She was about to speak when Doro beat her to it.

"Is Umberto coming this year?"

"Bachelors are hypocrites," she retorted. "I don't know," she then replied.

"You're enjoying all the disadvantages, Ginetta. You're marrying a bachelor who already leaves you alone. What will he do to you next?"

Half-seriously, Ginetta looked in front of her and shook her head.

"Usually, a husband used to be a bachelor," I observed calmly. "You have to get started somewhere."

But Ginetta was now talking about Umberto. She told us that he had written to say that the hyenas howled so much at night that it reminded him of children who didn't want to sleep. "Dear Ginetta," he said, "if our children make so much noise, I'll go to sleep in a hotel." Then he told her that the big difference between the desert and civilisation was that down there you couldn't sleep a wink because of the noise. "How silly," Ginetta laughed. "We're always joking."

The bends of the road among the pines, where the sea appeared, mixed with Ginetta's chatter to give me a pleasant feeling, a slight giddiness. It was as if the sea below was drawing us in. Even Doro walked more freely. Soon it was getting dark.

"Poor Mara," Ginetta said. "When will she be able to swim again?"

That evening we found the umbrella deserted, and the beach already empty. Ginetta and I went into the water and swam side by side as if in a race, not daring to separate in the silence of the empty sea. We came back without speaking, and between strokes I could see the high slope with the pine trees from which we had just descended. We touched the bottom; Ginetta emerged, glistening like a fish, and went to the cabin. Doro was finishing smoking the cigarette he had lit while waiting for me.

We went up to the villa together, where Clelia had already gone. That evening, at dinner, I heard that Mara had gone back to Sestri with Guido and that we would be alone and without a car for a few days. The news pleased me, as I loved spending the nights talking quietly.

"That stupid girl," Clelia said. "She could have waited until the end of the season before breaking her arm."

"Ginetta says we men are selfish," Doro observed.

"Do you like Ginetta?" Clelia asked me.

"She's a very healthy girl," I said. "Why? Is there something else?"

"Oh, nothing," said Clelia. "Doro claims that I looked like her when I was a girl." I declared that all girls look the same, and that you have to see them as women to make a judgement.

Clelia shrugged. "Who knows how you judge me," she muttered.

"I don't have enough information," I said. "Only Doro could judge you."

Doro unexpectedly began to joke about it, saying that a man in love has lost his ability to see clearly and that his judgement doesn't count. The way he spoke made him sound like Guido. I stared at him in astonishment. Fortunately, Clelia paid no attention and shrugged again, grumbling that we were all the same.

"What's the matter?" I exclaimed, laughing.

Nothing was the matter, and Clelia began to complain in a low voice that she felt like an old ruin, and the thought of her youth, or rather her childhood, when she was a schoolgirl going to her first dance and putting on long stockings for the first time, made her shudder. Doro listened absentmindedly, barely smiling. "I was too prudent as a child," Clelia said gloomily. "I thought that if Dad suddenly became poor from one day to the next or the kitchen burnt down, we wouldn't have anything to eat. I had stockpiled nuts and dried figs in the garden, waiting for us to become poor so that I could offer my provisions to Dad. I would have told Dad and Mum, 'Don't despair. Clelia thinks of everything. You've punished her, but now she forgives you — so don't do it again.' How stupid I was."

"We're all stupid at that age," I said.

"I used to believe everything they told me. I didn't dare put my face between the bars of the gate for fear someone might pass by and gouge out my eyes. But from the gate you could see the sea, and I had no other distraction, because they kept me shut up in the house all the time. I would sit on the bench and listen to the passers-by, to the sounds. When a siren went off in the harbour, I felt happy."

"Why are you telling him these things?" Doro said. "To put up with someone else's childhood memories, you have to be in love with them."

"But he loves me," Clelia said.

We chatted late into the night, and then we went out to look at the sea under the stars. The night was so clear that you could see the whiteness of the breaking waves under the promenade's railings. I said that at the end of the day, I didn't believe in all this water, that the sea made me feel like I was living under a bell jar. I described my olive tree as a kind of lunar vegetation, even when there was no moon.

Clelia, turning between me and Doro, exclaimed, "How beautiful! Let's go and see it."

But as we crossed the little square, we met some acquaintances, and we had to tell them about Mara. Clelia got caught up in the conversation and forgot about the olive tree, and everyone went back to the villa to play cards. A little annoyed, I left them, saying I was tired.

At the end of the square, I caught up with Berti, who hadn't managed to disappear into the darkness in time. I walked straight ahead, and it was Berti who spoke to me first.

"What's this following me for?" I said.

I had seen him an hour earlier in front of the villa, and he had always been hovering along the promenade, at some distance from us. The white jacket over his singlet was too conspicuous. He told me — emboldened by the darkness — that he had heard of an accident in the pinewood and wanted to make sure we were okay.

6

"As YOU CAN see, I'm alive," I told him. "Did you have to follow me all evening?"

He asked me if I was going to bed. We lingered under the olive tree, a black smudge in the darkness. "They said a woman got herself killed," Berti said.

"Are you interested in women too?"

Berti looked at my window, chin up. He turned briskly and said that an accident could make a holidaymaker leave, and he had thought that either I or my friends might be departing.

"Is she a relative of yours?" he asked.

I realised that evening that when he mentioned my friends he meant Clelia and Doro. He asked me again if Mara was their relative. The absurd suspicion that he might be interested in thirty-year-old Mara made me smile. I asked him if he knew her.

"No," he said. "Just asking."

I arranged to meet him on the beach the next day,

joking about his idea of reading together. "If you think you're going to meet girls through me, you're wrong. Seems to me you can do it on your own."

That night I sat by the window, smoking and thinking about Clelia's intimate revelations, annoyed by the thought that Ginetta would never confide such things in me. I was overcome by a familiar melancholy. I also remembered my conversation with Guido, which ended up depressing me. Luckily, I was by the sea, where the days don't count. "I'm here to enjoy myself," I thought.

The next day, Doro and I were sitting on top of the rocks, while below us Clelia was lying on her back, covering her eyes. The beach umbrella was deserted. We talked about Mara again and came to the conclusion that a beach is made up of women and, at most, children. If a man is missing, no one cares; but if a Mara is missing, the group falls apart. "Look," said Doro, "these umbrellas are like houses: they knit, eat, change, go visiting; the few husbands stay in the sun where their wives have put them. It is a republic of women."

"You could deduce that they were the ones who invented society."

At that moment, a swimmer reached the bottom of the rocks. He held on to them and raised his head out of the water. It was Berti.

I just watched him, without saying anything. Maybe he couldn't see me up there — when I come out of the water I can't see two steps ahead. He stayed propped against the rock, swaying with the waves. At the level of his forehead, a few palms away, Clelia lay motionless on her back. Berti's hair was dripping over his eyes and to hold himself in place his arms made those tentacle-like movements that still suggest swimming and instability. Then he suddenly broke free and swam on his back, circling a submerged rock where the sand was giving way to stone. He shouted something to me from there. I acknowledged him with a nod and went back to talking to Doro.

Later, when Clelia had snapped out of her reverie and the other girls and some acquaintances arrived, I cast my eyes around the beach and saw Berti standing between the cabins, reading a newspaper. This wasn't the first time, but that morning it was clear that he was waiting for me. I gestured for him to come over. I insisted. Berti moved, folding the newspaper without looking at us. He stopped at the foot of the rocks. I said to Doro, "This is the enterprising type I was telling you about." Doro looked up and smiled, then turned to his paintbox. It was now up to me to go down to Berti and say something.

To introduce a boy in black swimming trunks to girls coming and going in swimsuits and to men in robes is of little consequence, and overall acceptable. But Berti's serious and annoyed face irritated me; I felt ridiculous. "We all know each other here," I grumbled abruptly, and coming up to Ginetta as she went into the water, I said to her, "Wait for me."

When I got back to the shore — Ginetta had stayed in the water for over an hour — I saw him again, sitting on the sand between our umbrella and the next, hugging his knees.

I left him to it. I preferred to have a chat with Clelia. She was coming out of the cabin at that moment, putting on a white bolero over her swimsuit. I went up to her, and we greeted each other mockingly. We gradually moved away, talking, and when Berti had disappeared behind the umbrella, I felt better. We took our usual walk along the beach, between the foam and the scattered, noisy groups of people.

"I've been swimming with Ginetta," I said. "You're not getting in?"

From the first day I had offered to go into the water with her, out of politeness, but Clelia had stopped and looked at me with an ambiguous smile. "No, no," she had said. I looked at her in surprise. "No, no, I swim by myself." There was no way around it. She explained that she did everything in public, but in the sea, she had to be alone. "But it's strange." "It's strange, but that's the way it is." She swam well, so it wasn't out of embarrassment. It was just a decision she had made. "The company of the sea is enough for me. I don't want anyone. I have nothing in life that's only mine. At least leave me the sea." She swam away without disturbing the water, and when she returned, I was waiting for her on the sand. I returned to the subject, and Clelia responded to my protests with a half-smile.

"Not even with Doro?" I asked.

"Not even with Doro."

This morning, we joked about her mysterious swim as we skirted bodies, laughed at potbellies and criticised women. "That red beach umbrella," said Clelia, "do you know who's under it?" On the beach chair you could make out a bony nakedness covered by a two-piece swimsuit, bra and pants. She was unevenly tanned; her bare stomach showed the outline of a previous, regular swimsuit. Her toenails and fingernails were blood red. A beautiful pink towel hung from the back of the beach chair. "She's Guido's girlfriend," Clelia whispered, laughing. "He brings her along and keeps her hidden, and when he meets her, he kisses her hand and exchanges pleasantries with her." Then she took my arm and leaned over.

"Why are you men so vulgar?"

"It seems to me that Guido has all sorts of tastes," I said. "When it comes to vulgarity, he has plenty of it."

"But no," Clelia said, "it's that woman who's vulgar. Poor thing, he's very fond of me."

I began to explain to her that nothing is vulgar in itself, but that we make things vulgar by how we speak or think, but Clelia was already looking elsewhere and laughing at a little red cap that a tiny boy was wearing.

We walked like this to the end of the beach, stopping to smoke on the rocks. Then we walked back, numbed by the harsh sun, and I was looking around with little interest when I saw Berti walking away from our beach umbrella — suntanned back and swimming trunks — and talking with an agitated air to a petite woman in a quirky floral dressing gown, high-heeled sandals and shiny, powdered cheeks. Just then, Clelia shouted something to Doro, raising her arm, and they both turned. Berti ran off in a hurry as soon as he saw us, while the little woman hobbled after him, casual and mocking, calling him by name.

"That geisha who was chasing you," I said to him when he came looking for me at the trattoria, "was she by any chance the lady you brought home the other day?"

Berti smiled indifferently over his cigarette.

"I see you have good company," I continued. "Why are you looking for more? Luckily I didn't introduce you to those young ladies."

Berti stared at me, the way you do when you pretend to think about something. "It's not my fault," he said abruptly, "if I ran into her. Apologise to your friends on my behalf."

Then I changed the subject and asked him if his parents knew about these adventures. With his usual vague smile he said calmly that this woman was worth more than many girls from good families. Besides, the hard life that all women like her had to lead was to the advantage of the respectable ones.

"What do you mean?"

"Yes, all men are happy to go to prostitutes, and there they let off steam and no longer bother the other women. Therefore they should respect them."

"All right," I told him. "But then why do you run away and feel ashamed of her?"

"Me?" Berti stammered. It was a different matter, he explained: he felt revulsion towards women, and it made him angry that all men lived just for that. Women were stupid and affected: men's infatuation made them necessary; all you had to do was agree to stop chasing them, and that would take away all their arrogance.

"Berti, Berti," I said to him, "you're a hypocrite too."

He looked at me in surprise. "Using someone," I continued, "and then cutting them off, that's not right." Then I saw him smile and ostentatiously crush his cigarette. In his mellowest tone, he said that he had not used this woman, but — he smiled — this woman had used him. She was alone, bored by the seaside; they had bumped into each other on the beach — she herself had begun to joke and make a fuss. "You see," he said to me, "I didn't say no, because I felt sorry for her. She has a handbag with a mirror that's completely broken. I understand her. She's just looking for company and doesn't want any money. She says you don't work at the seaside. But she's mean. She is like all women, who use mockery to make a man look stupid."

We went back home through the deserted streets of two o'clock in the afternoon. I had decided not to give the boy any more advice: he was the kind of person you had to let do his thing to see how far he would go. I asked him if he hadn't by chance brought this woman, this lady, with him from Turin. "You're crazy," he replied sharply. But all his impulsiveness left him when I asked him who had taught him to apologise for things that no one cared about. "When?" he stammered. "Didn't you just ask me to apologise to my friends on your behalf?" I said.

He explained that, as I was with my friends, he was sorry that we had seen him with that woman. "There are people," he said, "that you're ashamed to make a fool of yourself in front of."

"Like who, for example?"

He was silent for a moment. "Your friends," he stammered casually.

He left me at the bottom of the stairs and walked away under the sun. Since Doro rested during those scorching hours, and I couldn't sleep during the day, I pretended to go back inside just to get rid of Berti. And now began the daily tedium of those hot and empty hours. I wandered around the village as usual, but there wasn't a corner I didn't know. Then I took the road to the villa, eager to speak to Clelia. But it was still very early, and I brooded for a long time, sitting on a low wall behind some plants that stood out against the sea. Among other things, I thought for the first time that someone who did not know Clelia well, seeing us walking and laughing together, would say that there was more between us than just friendship.

I found Clelia in the garden, lying in a wicker chair in the shade. She seemed pleased to see me and started talking. She told me that Doro was tired of always painting the sea and wanted to stop. A smile escaped me. "Your Guido will be happy," I said. "Why?" I then had to explain to her that, according to Guido, Doro thought more about painting than he did about her, and that was the reason for their arguments.

"Arguments?" Clelia said, frowning.

I grew impatient. "Come on, Clelia, you don't expect me to believe that you haven't been fighting a little. Remember that evening when you begged me to keep him company and distract him?"

Clelia listened, half-frowning and shaking her head in denial. "I never said anything," she muttered.

"I don't remember." She smiled. "I don't want to remember. And you, don't be rude."

"What the hell," I said. "The first day I was here. We were coming back from that trip where we were shot at..."

"What a beauty!" Clelia cried. "And that white man fooling around?"

I couldn't help smiling and Clelia said, "You all take me at my word. You all remember what I say. And you interrogate me, you want to know." She frowned again. "I feel like I'm back at school."

"For me…" I muttered.

"People should never remember what I say. I talk and talk because I have a tongue in my mouth, because I don't know how to be alone. You shouldn't take me seriously either, it's not worth it."

"Oh Clelia," I said, "are we tired of life?"

"Oh no, it's beautiful," she said, laughing.

Then I said I could no longer understand poor Doro. Why did he want to give up painting? He was doing so well.

Clelia became pensive and said that if she hadn't been what she was — a spoiled child who didn't know how to do anything — she would have painted the sea, she loved it so much and it was her thing; and not just the sea, but the houses, the people, the steep steps, all of Genoa. "I like it so much," she said.

"Maybe that's why Doro ran away. For the same reason. He likes the hills."

"Could be. But he says his village is only beautiful in his memory. I couldn't be like that. I don't have anything else of my own."

We sat, facing each other across the small table, waiting for Doro. Clelia began to tell me again about her childhood, joking a lot about the naivety of that life, about the closed environment of old men who wanted to turn her into a countess and tossed her around between three houses — a shop, a *palazzo* and a villa. What she liked was the triangle of streets that connected them, that crossed the whole town. Her uncle's palazzo was an old building with frescoes and brocades, full of glass like a museum. Seen from the street, it overlooked the sea, and it had large stained-glass windows. As a child, Clelia said, it was a nightmare to enter that hallway and spend the after-noon in the gloomy semi-darkness of the rooms. Beyond the roof, there was the sea, there was the air, there was the busy street. She had to wait for her mother to finish whispering to the old female servant; and constantly, tormented by boredom, she would raise her eyes to the dark paintings, where there were flashes of moustaches, cardinals' hats, and the faded cheeks of ageless dolls.

"You see how silly I am," Clelia said, "when the palazzo was almost ours, I couldn't bear it; now that we're poor and broke, I'd give anything to have it back."

Before Doro appeared on the balcony, Clelia also told me that her mother didn't want her to stay in the shop where her father worked, because it wasn't nice for a girl like her to hear arguments behind the counter and learn so many rude words. But the shop was full of things and had glittering display cases — the same objects that filled the palazzo — and there were always people coming and going; Clelia was happy to see her father content. She used to ask him why they didn't also sell the paintings and lamps from the palazzo, so they wouldn't go into ruin. "I had a prudent childhood," she told me, smiling. "I used to wake up at night terrified that Dad had become poor."

"Why were you so afraid?"

Clelia said that she was drenched in fear in those years. She had her first feelings of love in front of a painting of Saint Sebastian the Martyr, a naked young man, all bloodied and peeling, with arrows piercing his stomach. The saint's sad and loving eyes made her ashamed to look at him, and for her, love was represented by that scene.

"Why am I telling you this?" she said.

Shortly afterwards, Doro appeared on the balcony, carefully wiping his neck dry. He nodded at me and went back inside on his way down. I asked Clelia if she had since changed her mind about love.

"Of course," she said.

7

WHEN I CAME back to my room at night I used to stand by the window and smoke. People think it helps you meditate, but the truth is that smoking disperses your thoughts like fog, and at best you fantasise, which is very different from thinking. Ideas and discoveries, on the other hand, come unexpectedly: at the dinner table, while swimming in the sea or while discussing a completely different topic. Doro knew of my habit of fading out for a moment in the middle of a conversation to follow an unexpected idea with my eyes. He used to do the same, and in the past we had often walked together, each of us ruminating in silence. But now his silences — like mine — seemed distracted, alienated; in short, odd. I had only been by the seaside for a few days, and it felt like a century — yet nothing had happened. But when I came back at night, I had the feeling that the whole day that had passed — the mundane day on the beach — was waiting for me to make some sort of effort to clarify things, to make sense of it.

The day after Mara's accident, when I saw our friend Guido again in his bloody car, I intuited in the few seconds it took me to cross the street to shake his hand more than I had in a whole night of pipe-smoking. I had a hunch, that is, that Clelia's intimate revelations were an unconscious defence against Guido's vulgarity — a man who was, nevertheless, polite and gentlemanly. Guido sat there, tanned and ruddy, holding out his hand and flashing his teeth in greeting. Guido was rich and bovine. Clelia reacted only furtively, which made me think she took him seriously and in fact resembled him. Who knows at what further insights I would have arrived if Guido hadn't started laughing, forcing me to say something. I got into his car, and he took me to the café where everyone was at that hour.

While they were talking about Mara, I concentrated on entertaining my thoughts, wondering if Doro understood Clelia's regrets as well as I did, and why it didn't bother him that Clelia had no secrets even from me. In the meantime, they had both arrived, and after the first few words Guido told Clelia he had been thinking about her while driving through Genoa. Clelia called him mean. It was a joke, but it was enough to make me suspect that she had also shared her childhood secrets with Guido in the past, and that didn't sit well with me.

After dinner, Guido joined us at the villa. He looked very cheerful and brought Ginetta along in his car. While Doro and Guido talked about their work, I listened to Clelia and Ginetta and thought about Doro's remark, on the way down from the mountain, that it was characteristic of those who marry to live with more than one woman. But was Ginetta a woman? Her frowning smile and the intrusiveness of some of her opinions made her seem more like a sexless teenager. I couldn't understand how Clelia could have resembled her as a girl. There was a contained, restrained mischievousness in Ginetta, which was sometimes unleashed through her whole body. She certainly wouldn't share intimate secrets with her friends, and yet, watching her speak, you felt that nothing remained hidden in her depths. Her unassuming grey eyes had the clarity of air.

They were discussing some scandal — I don't remember the details — but I remember the girl defending the person involved and appealing to Doro, interrupting him at random, and Clelia repeating, very gently, that it was not a matter of morality but of taste.

"But they are getting married," said Ginetta.

It wasn't a solution, Clelia replied. Getting married was a choice, not a remedy, and a choice that should be made calmly.

"Damn it, it will be a choice," Guido interjected. "After all the experiments they've done."

Ginetta didn't smile and countered that if the purpose of marriage was having a family, it was good that they thought about it right away.

"But the purpose is not just family," Doro said. "It is to prepare an environment for the family."

"Better a child without an environment than an environment without children," Ginetta declared. Then she blushed and met my gaze. Clelia got up to serve us some liqueur.

After that we played cards. Late at night Guido drove us home. After dropping Ginetta off in front of the garage, we walked back to the hotel. I would have preferred to walk alone, but Guido, who had said little all evening and played cards with aggressive carelessness, asked me to keep him company. I talked to him again about Mara. Guido responded with little enthusiasm: Mara was in good hands and out of danger. When we arrived at his hotel, he walked straight on.

We reached the entrance to my alley in silence, and I was about to stop. Guido walked on a few steps, then turned around and said casually: "Let them wait. Come with me up to the station."

I asked who would be waiting for me, and Guido said nonchalantly that damn it, I had to have someone to keep me company.

"There's no one," I replied. "I'm single and alone."

Then Guido muttered something, and we were off again.

Who would be waiting for me? I asked again. Perhaps that youth from the beach?

"No, no, *Professore*, I meant a relationship... an affair."

"Why? Have you seen me in company?"

"I'm not saying that. But after all, sometimes you have to unwind."

"I'm here to relax," I explained. "And I unwind by being alone."

"Okay," Guido said absent-mindedly.

We were standing in the small square in front of the café when I spoke. "And do you have company?" I said.

Guido raised his head. "I do," he said bluntly. "I do. We are not all saints. And it costs me an arm and a leg."

"Ingeniere," I exclaimed, "but you hide her very well."

Guido smiled smugly. "That's what's costing me an arm and a leg. Two bills, two private beaches, two tables. Believe me, a lover costs more than a wife."

"You should get married then," I said.

Guido flashed his gold teeth. "It would still be double the cost. You don't know women. A girl-friend, as long as she has hope, keeps quiet. She has everything to gain. But the poor man who has a wife is at her mercy."

"Then marry your girlfriend."

"You must be joking. That's what people do when they're old."

I left him outside the hotel, promising him to meet the lady the next day. He shook my hand expansively. When I got back to my place, I thought of Berti and looked around, but this time he wasn't there.

The next day, I wrote until the sun was high, and then I wandered the streets, still mulling over the ideas of the night before, which now, in the bustle and brightness of the day, seemed to me faded and disjointed. I wanted to go to the beach, thinking that everyone would be there by now.

But at the entrance to the resort I found Guido, this time in a brown robe, who immediately grabbed me, and we walked, as if by silent agreement, towards a certain beach umbrella. When we arrived, Guido broke into a spontaneous smile and exclaimed: "Nina, darling, how did you sleep? Allow me" — and he told her my name. I touched the fingers of that skinny hand, and in the glare and the obstruction of the umbrella, I saw mainly her long and tanned legs, and the intricate sandals they ended in. She had risen to sit on the deck chair and looked at me with hard eyes, as devoid of substance as the voice she directed towards Guido.

We exchanged a few pleasantries, I asked about her swimming; she told me she only bathed in the warm water towards evening; she chuckled a few times at my little jokes and held out her hand as I said goodbye, inviting me to come back. Guido stayed with her.

I reached the rocks and saw Berti sitting, his back against a boulder, engaged in conversation with Ginetta's sixteen-year-old friend, while Doro lay on the sand between them, leaving them alone. Clelia was in the water.

8

ONE MORNING DORO explained to me why he was tired of painting. He had taken me by the arm, and we walked slowly away from the village, along the coastal road overlooking the sea.

"If I could be a boy again," he told me, " I'd dedicate myself solely to painting. I'd run away from home and slam the door behind me, but it would be a decisive move."

I liked that passion and told him he wouldn't have married Clelia in that case. Doro laughed and said that Clelia was the only thing he hadn't got wrong; she was indeed a beautiful vocation. However, he said, it wasn't the silly pictures he painted in his spare time that upset him; it was that he had lost the passion and the desire to discuss things with me.

"What things?"

He stared at me intensely, refusing to back down, and said that if I saw it that way, he would stop complaining, because I was getting older too, and it seemed to happen to everyone.

"Maybe," I said, "but if you've lost the will to talk about things, it's not my fault."

I realised that I was annoyed and that it was ridiculous, but in the meantime, I remained silent, and Doro let go of my arm. I looked out at the sea below us, and a thought crossed my mind: did his arguments with Clelia consist of similar nonsense?

But then Doro started talking again, in the same carefree voice as before, and I realised that he hadn't even noticed my annoyance. I replied to him in an indifferent tone, but the resentment inside me grew into real, authentic anger.

"You still haven't explained why you quarrelled with Clelia," I finally said.

But Doro evaded me again. At first, he didn't understand what I was referring to, then he looked at me sideways and said, "Are you still thinking about it? You're stubborn! It happens every day between husband and wife."

That same day I told Clelia, who was complaining about a boring novel, that in such cases, the fault lay with the reader. Clelia looked up and smiled. "It happens to all of you," she said. "You come here to rest, and you become impertinent."

"Who's all of us?"

"Even Guido. But at least Guido has the excuse that his girlfriend is tormenting him. You don't."

I shrugged, with a sneering grimace. When I told her that I had met this lady, Clelia's face blushed with delight and she almost clapped her hands, begging: "Tell me, tell me. What is she like?"

All I knew was that Guido had half a mind to get rid of her — by dumping her on me, for instance. I said this in the reserved tone that Clelia liked, and I saw that she was pleased. "He complains that she costs him too much," I added. "Then why doesn't he marry her?"

"That's the last thing we need!" Clelia said. "But the woman is stupid. Her intelligence shows in her willingness to be kept in the closet like a box. Do you like her?"

"I've only seen her legs so far. Who is she? A dancer?"

"A cashier," Clelia said. "A witch that everyone in Genoa knew, before Guido fell into her clutches."

"So she must be cunning."

"It doesn't take much with Guido," Clelia smiled.

"I think she is pretending to be obedient to trap him better," I said. "It's a good sign when a woman lets herself be kept in the closet. It means she already considers herself at home."

"If you think it's a good sign," Clelia said, frowning.

"But what better option does he have than marrying her?"

"No, no," Clelia became indignant. "I wouldn't let him set foot in my house again."

"Would you rather a brute like him marry a Clelia or a Ginetta?" I glanced at her to gauge her reaction, but she let the word pass. "What an injustice," Clelia said. "That a girl should be defenceless against you guys. Those women who take you for a ride are absolutely right."

One afternoon, Guido actually came to visit me at home. He appeared at the door with an apologetic smile, saying he didn't want to disturb my reading. I let him in, embarrassed by the rickety iron bed, and invited him to sit by the window. He fanned himself with his hat and then asked me to apologise to Doro and Clelia on his behalf, because he couldn't come and pick us up in the car. He had something on.

That evening on the beach, we made some disparaging remarks about Guido. The most resentful were the girls, who had been looking forward to the outing. Berti, now a regular among us, seemed to be the only one who didn't care. I heard him say to Ginetta that people came to the sea to swim, after all, not for sightseeing.

"So," I said, sitting down next to him on the sand, "you don't think any more about reading?"

"No, I'd still love to do it," he said to me.

"Maybe with these girls."

He looked at me resentfully. "Me?" he said. Sitting under the rocks, he really looked annoyed. Yet just earlier, when I had seen him, he was holding his own against everyone with a condescending, disinclined air.

"You're not going to tell me that we disgust you too. You came looking for us."

Berti smiled. Ginetta walked past us, adjusting her cap, ready to swim. From where I was sitting, I watched her walking slowly while covering her ear, and she seemed very tall to me, more than a woman. Berti looked down at his knees and grumbled: "They get on my nerves. Who can understand girls?"

Doro stopped in front of us, about to throw himself on the sand. "This is the student," I said. I introduced them. They shook hands, on their knees.

Then Doro started talking to me about I don't know what, in one of those bizarre and brusque moods that we used to have as students. It was clear that Berti had nothing to do with it. On one side I listened to Doro, on the other I kept an eye on my young friend.

Berti then asked out of the blue: "Ingeniere, will you be staying long?"

Doro looked at him askance and did not answer. Berti waited, his face flushed despite his tan. After a long silence, I said that I was leaving at the end of August. But Doro, unrelenting, didn't say a word. All three of us looked out to sea, where Ginetta got into the water and Clelia unexpectedly emerged. We watched her approach, and I didn't know if I should smile. Then she grimaced at us, having slipped on the pebbles.

"Come on, the sea is yours," she shouted, waving to us, and headed for the beach umbrella. Doro had got up. "Shall we go for a walk?" he said to me. I got up, barely glancing at Berti. He was still staring stoically at the horizon.

Later, fresh and rested, we sat around the umbrella, Clelia smoking a cigarette and I smoking my pipe.

"I wonder where Berti has gone," I said. Doro didn't move. He was lying between us, looking up at the sky.

"You two are real friends," Clelia said. "You're inseparable."

"I'm just a screen for his love affairs," I said. "There's a woman who would be jealous otherwise."

Clelia liked these stories, and I had to tell her everything about the incident and the conversation we had in the trattoria. Doro remained silent, his eyes fixed on the sky.

9

THE NEXT TIME I SAW Berti in the trattoria, he looked grumpy. It seemed that he had only come in because he had nothing better to do. He said he wanted to come over in the afternoon to read together.

"Don't you like girls anymore?" I said.

"Which girls? I hate them," he replied.

"You don't mean you want the engineer's company?"

He asked me if Doro was really my friend. I replied that yes, he and his wife were the best friends I had.

"His wife?"

He didn't know that Clelia was Doro's wife. His eyes sparkled. "Really?" he repeated, lowering them with that impassive look of annoyance he used to have when he was serious.

"What did you think?" I muttered. "That she was a dancer?"

Berti fiddled with the tablecloth and let me speak.

Then he looked at me with two bright, naive eyes, the eyes of a boy, and asked me again if he could come up to see me that afternoon.

"Is no one coming to see you?" he said. It was obvious that he was thinking of Clelia.

"What is it?" I said. "You hate women and yet you blush when you think of them?"

Berti replied with some nonsense, and then we fell silent. Finally, we got up. On the way, he didn't say much, but he answered my questions animatedly, with the air of someone who speaks at random, simply because a thought occurs to him. I stopped under the olive tree to speak to the landlady for a moment, and he waited for me at the foot of the stairs, looking at the smooth stone balustrade, caressing it, with a smile on his lips that was at once tender and contemptuous. "Come upstairs," I said when I reached him.

When we were upstairs, he went to the window and leaned against it, watching me as I walked around the room.

"Professore, I'm happy," he blurted out suddenly, as I turned my back to him and rinsed my mouth.

I asked him why, and he replied with a gesture, as if to say, "Just because."

We did not read that afternoon either. He began to tell me that from time to time he felt an urge to work, a longing, a desire to do something — not so much to study but to have a position of responsibility, of effort, to really throw himself into it day and night, to become a man like us, like me. "Then you should work," I told him. Then he told me he didn't understand why people valued youth so much: he wished he was already thirty — so much the better. The years in between were just stupid.

"But all years are stupid. It's only when they're over that they become interesting."

No, Berti said, he didn't find anything interesting in his fifteen or his seventeen years; he was glad they were over.

I told him that the beauty of his age was that foolishness didn't matter, and that was precisely thanks to what was bothering him: that they were considered just boys.

He looked at me and smiled.

"So the things I do aren't foolish?"

"That depends," I said, "If you annoy the wives of my friends, it will certainly be foolishness, as well as rudeness."

"I don't annoy anyone," he protested.

"We'll see about that."

He confessed during our conversation that he had stupidly thought the lady was my friend's mistress. The discovery that she was actually his wife pleased him because he was too angry that women, just because they were women, would sell themselves to the first bidder. "There are days when the world, life itself, seems to me like one big brothel."

At that moment, he was interrupted by a familiar shrill voice coming from the street, the voice of an embittered woman snapping back at our landlady. We exchanged glances. Berti fell silent and lowered his eyes. I understood that it was the woman from the beach, the one we jokingly called his lover. Berti didn't move.

The landlady said, "He's not here. I don't know anything." The other shouted obscenities and declared that no one had ever disrespected her, and that not even holy water could cleanse the landlady's face.

When they became silent and someone walked away, I waited for Berti to speak, but he just stared blankly into space with a hardened and distracted expression and remained silent.

When he left, I told him to make sure it did not happen again. I cut it short and closed the door.

He didn't come to the rocks that evening. Guido came over, wiping off his sweat. Clelia asked him teasingly when we were going to dance up on the hill again.

"Did you hear that?" he said to Doro. "Your wife feels like dancing."

"I don't," Doro replied.

Clelia was telling me about a small balcony in her uncle's old palazzo that had come to her mind that evening, and how she wished she could find herself there. Guido listened to her for a while, then said that

I was just the right man to appreciate these voices from the past.

Clelia smiled uncomfortably and replied that when it came to discussing the present, she expected him to take the lead. We looked at Guido, who winked — at me, I think — and replied to Clelia that she should at least tell us something interesting — her first ball, for example — a woman's first ball is always full of surprises.

"No, no," said Clelia, "we want to hear about your first ball. Or even the last one, the one last night."

Doro stood up and said, "Take it easy. I'm going for a swim."

"That's right," I said. "People always talk about girls' first balls. What about the boys? What happens to future Guidos the first time they embrace a girl?"

"There is no first time," Clelia said. "Future Guidos didn't start at any particular time. They were already doing it before they were born."

We went on like this until Doro returned. Clelia liked these aggressive jokes, mixing in a teasing undertone, a touch of malice that — perhaps I'm wrong — Guido didn't always grasp. Or rather, he seemed to put up with it, preoccupied elsewhere, but his grudging compliance in joining the game made me smile.

I said, "You two seem like husband and wife."

"How rude!" Clelia said.

"Can you do anything but joke with a woman like Clelia?" Guido said.

"There's only one man Clelia doesn't joke with," I replied in my turn.

"Of course," Clelia said.

Doro turned around and threw himself on the sand in the fading sunlight. After a while, Guido got up and said he was going to the bar. He walked away between the closed umbrella poles, navigating the bumps and swerves of the evening crowd. A short distance away, Ginetta and other young people were noisily greeting an incoming boat. The three of us remained silent; I listened to the muffled thud and chatter.

"Do you know, Clelia," I said suddenly, "that my student decided to change his life after seeing you?"

Doro looked up. Clelia's eyes widened.

"He has dismissed that lover of his, and he denigrates all women. It's an unmistakable sign."

"Thanks," Clelia murmured.

Doro lay down again. "Since Doro is here," I continued, "I might as well say it. He's in love with you."

Clelia smiled, without moving. "I'm sorry about that... Is there anything I can do?"

A smile escaped me.

"With so many girls out there looking," Clelia said, "it's annoying."

"But why?" I said. "He's happy. Happier than we are. You should see him caressing the tree trunks and going into a trance."

"If he takes it like that," Clelia said.

Doro turned over on the sand. "Oh, stop it," he said.

We told him to shut up because he had nothing to do with it. Clelia looked at the sand for a moment without speaking. "But is it really true?" she asked suddenly.

Laughing, I reassured her. "What does this fool see in me?" she asked. She looked at me suspiciously. "You're all fools," she said.

I repeated that my student was happy and that was enough, and that I would be happy to be a fool under those conditions.

Then Clelia smiled and said, "It's true. It's like when I used to stand on the balcony and, instead of studying, throw paper balls at the necks of passers-by. Once a gentleman was waiting for me downstairs and gave me a fright. He wanted to know what I had written to him. It was a Latin assignment."

Doro laughed, lying face up on the sand.

"And that gentleman was Guido," I said.

Clelia glared at me. What did I have against Guido, she asked. I felt bad. "I know him," I told her.

"Guido doesn't do things like that," Clelia said. "Guido respects women."

10

GUIDO HESITANTLY INVITED me to go to the night-club in his car one evening. "Nina will be there. You don't mind, do you?" He glanced at Berti, who had stayed a few steps behind to let me talk, and looked at me questioningly. I asked him to bring Berti along as well — a spirited young man who could dance, which was more than I could do. Guido frowned and said, "Of course." Then I introduced them.

It was an evening of silence. Berti had thought he would find Clelia there, but instead, he ended up dancing with Nina, who eyed him up and down and was at a loss for words. We, sitting at the table, remained silent, following the couples with our eyes. It wasn't that Guido wanted to get rid of Nina; the casual remark he made to me seemed more like a way of letting off steam. "I'm at an age, Professore, where I can't change my life, but if Nina wanted to have some fun and find an environment — a circle of friends that would be good for her — I would view it favourably."

"You just have to tell her."

"No," said Guido. "She feels lonely. You see, a man has friends, relationships to maintain. He can't always devote his time to her."

"Wouldn't a frank explanation suffice?" I suggested.

"With other women, yes, but not with her. A girlfriend, an old girlfriend, you understand... a demanding woman, you know what I mean?"

Then Nina danced a bit with him, and Berti smoked cigarettes at the table and looked around. He asked me if that lady was Guido's wife.

"Not that one," I told him. "She's from the world you imagine. Who are you looking for?"

"No one."

"My friends aren't coming. When this lady is around, they won't come."

That night, on the steps under the olive tree, I asked him if he liked Nina, and when he grimaced, I retorted that it would be a favour to Guido if he entertained her a little. "But if he's tired of her, why doesn't he leave her?" said Berti. "Try asking him," I said.

Berti didn't ask him, and instead, the next evening, having caught wind of the news that Clelia, Guido and I were going to dance, he walked up there — I don't know if he'd had dinner. We saw him go in between the tables and sit at the back. He had his soft drink in front of him and he threw away his cigarette. But he didn't move.

As it happened, Ginetta wasn't in the group. It was clear to me — by now I felt I could read his mind — that Berti was hoping Ginetta's presence would help him start dancing. Guido, rejuvenated by his evening of freedom, looked around contentedly and gave him a distracted nod. Berti got up and came towards us. Being a coward, I kept my eyes on the ground. "How is the *Signora*?" Berti asked.

Clelia broke the embarrassment with an irrepressible laugh. Then Guido replied, "We're all fine," with a tone and a vague gesture that made us all smile, except for Berti, who blushed.

He stayed there for a while, watching us, and I couldn't resist; I said, glancing at Clelia, "This is Berti, that you've already heard about." Doro, with a look of disinterest, gestured for him to sit down and muttered, "Stay with us."

Of course, I was the one who had to entertain him. Berti, sitting on the edge of the chair, glanced at us patiently. I asked him what he was doing up here alone, and Berti replied with a grimace, twitching as if listening to the orchestra. "My friend tells me you've given up studying," Doro said suddenly. "What are you doing now? Working?"

"I'm unemployed," Berti replied with some aggression.

"My friend says you're having fun," Doro continued anyway. "Is there someone with you?"

Berti simply said no. We all fell silent. Clelia, half-facing the orchestra, turned her head and said: "Do you dance, Berti?"

I was grateful to her for these words. Berti managed to look at her steadily and nodded. "It's a pity Ginetta and Luisella didn't come," Clelia said. "You know them, don't you?" Without taking his eyes off her, Berti replied that he did. "Won't you dance with me?" Clelia said.

As they walked away, none of us said anything. Guido stirred restlessly as he picked up a teaspoon, and meanwhile my eyes met Doro's. I think he read an uneasy question on my face, because while I was embarrassed and about to look away, I saw him furrow his brow and smile faintly.

"What's wrong?" Guido said as he stood up.

Clelia and Berti came back almost immediately. I'm not sure if the orchestra had finished quicker than usual or if my unease had distracted me. They returned, and Clelia said something — I don't remember what — the kind of comment she might have made when getting out of a taxi. Berti followed her like a shadow.

They danced together once more during the evening. I think it was Clelia who had encouraged him with a glance. Berti got up without saying a word and waited for Clelia to join him, barely looking at her. During the intermissions, when I was sitting at the table with either Doro or Guido, one of us would occasionally speak to Berti, and he would respond condescendingly, in monosyllables. Guido danced a lot with Clelia and came back to the table with his eyes sparkling. Then we all stayed at the table for a while, chatting. Berti tried not to look at Clelia too much and seemed bored, absorbed in the orchestra. He didn't speak. Then Guido said to him:

"Are you retaking your exams this year?"

"No," Berti muttered calmly.

"Because you look like someone about to take his exams, not like an educated person."

Berti smiled stupidly. Clelia smiled again. Doro didn't move. Seconds passed, and no one spoke. Guido gave us a sideways glance and muttered something. More offensive than anything else was the half-sneer of contempt he directed at Berti. As if to say, "It's over. Let's forget about it."

Berti said nothing. He still smiled vaguely. Suddenly, Clelia said, "Would you like to dance?" I raised my head. Berti had got up.

Clelia returned to the table alone, nodding calmly to someone she knew. She sat down with a tired expression, almost a frown, and muttered, without looking at us, "I hope you'll be more amusing now." At that moment, a couple of friends emerged from the dim light and distracted us.

Back in the car, Clelia replied to my half-question that Berti hadn't said a word while they were dancing. Guido, on the other hand, had plenty to say when we were left alone, on our way to the bar for the last time. He explained that he couldn't stand boys and that he couldn't tolerate them having the air of lecturing him. "They have to live too," I said, "and learn from experience." "First let them go through as much as we have," Guido retorted stubbornly.

Nina was waiting for him at the bar. I was expecting her. She was sitting in front of a low table, her chin resting on her fist, following the trail of smoke from her cigarette. She greeted us with a nod, and while Guido ordered at the bar, she asked me, in her rough and uneven voice, without taking her hand away, why I didn't come around more often.

"What about last night?" I said.

"You don't dance, you don't sunbathe, you don't eat out with anyone — why don't you join us? Oh, Guido's friends: what does this woman have that she can seduce you all? Don't tell me it's the engineer's company you're after."

"I'm not saying anything," I stammered.

It was so warm that night that it was a shame to go back inside. I wondered if Berti was waiting for me at the bottom of the stairs. He had probably gone to sit on the beach to wallow in his shame. I didn't really want to see him. Back in my room, I stood at the window for a long time.

The next day, Berti called me from the street. Our alley was still all in shadow. He shouted for me to come to the sea with him. After a moment of silence, he asked if he could come up. He entered with an aggressive stride, his eyes shining and tired. "Do you think now is the right time?" I said. He looked as if he hadn't slept and told me so almost immediately, in a casual tone, as if he were bragging about it. "Come to the sea, Professore," he insisted. "There is no one there."

I had a letter to write. "Professore," he said after a little silence, "All you have to do is turn night into day and then everything becomes beautiful."

I looked up from the paper. "Troubles at your age are very minor."

Berti smiled with a certain harshness. "Why should I have any troubles?" he asked, looking down.

"I thought you had a fight," I said.

"With who?" he interrupted.

"All right then," I grumbled.

"Come to the sea, Professore," Berti said. "The sea is huge."

11

I TOLD HIM I was going there with my friends later and asked him to leave me alone. He left with a look that was somewhere between serious and annoyed, and I immediately felt sorry for having treated him so badly. But never mind, I concluded, you're learning at his expense. I have learned something.

I met Guido at the bar. He was wearing his usual open collar shirt and white trousers, and the fake masculinity of his tan made me smile. Guido shook my hand with a smile and lifted his eyes to the rooftops, their expression between sly and stern. "What a day," he said. It was a truly enchanting sky and morning. "Have a Marsala, Professore. Last night, eh?" He winked, I don't know why, and wouldn't let me go. "And what's beautiful Clelia up to?" he said.

"I've just come from my room."

"You're always so proper, Professore."

We started walking. He asked me if I was staying at the seaside for much longer. "I'm beginning to have enough," I said. "Too many complications."

Guido wasn't listening to me, or perhaps he didn't understand.

"You have no company," he said.

"I have my friends."

"That's not enough. I have the same friends, but I wouldn't be in such good shape this morning if I'd slept in a single bed."

Since I was silent, he explained that he also enjoyed Clelia's company, but that smelling the roast was not the same as eating it.

"And the roast would be?"

Guido burst out laughing. "There are women of flesh," he said, "and women of air. A puff after lunch is good for you. But you must have eaten first."

I told him that honestly, I was staying at the seaside for Doro.

"By the way," I said, "he doesn't paint anymore."

"It's about time," Guido retorted.

But neither Clelia nor Doro came to the beach that morning. Gisella and the others knew nothing about it. By midday I was getting impatient, and taking advantage of the fact that they were talking about a boat trip, I put my clothes back on and walked up to the villa. There was nobody in the street. I was approaching the gate when Doro appeared on the gravel with an elderly gentleman wearing a Panama hat and carrying a walking stick, who walked leisurely towards the road, listening to words I couldn't hear and nodding in response. When we were alone, Doro looked at me with comically uneasy eyes.

"What's happening?" I said.

"What's happening is that Clelia is pregnant."

Before rejoicing, I waited for Doro to give me the cue. We walked back up the driveway towards the steps. Doro looked incredulous and amused. "So you're happy," I said. "I want to see how it ends first," he grumbled. "It's the first time it's ever happened to me."

Clelia then came out of the room and asked who was there. She smiled at me, almost apologetically, and brought her handkerchief to her mouth. "Don't I disgust you?" she said.

Then we talked about the doctor, who had spoken extensively about responsibility and wanted to come back with I don't know what instruments to make a scientific diagnosis. "What a nutcase," Clelia said.

"No way," Doro blurted out. "Today we're taking the train and going to Genoa. De Luca has to examine you."

Clelia looked at me, resigned. "You see," she said. "Paternity has already started. He's in charge."

I said I was sorry she had to interrupt her time at the seaside, but that it was a good thing after all.

"And you think I'm not sorry?" grumbled Clelia.

Doro was counting on his fingers. "It will be more or less…"

"Stop it," Clelia said.

Instead of taking the train, they went in Guido's car. Doro, who accompanied me to the village, confided in me that he felt a certain disgust at the idea of talking to people about it, and that he would have preferred a sprain or a fracture. He chattered with great volubility, joking about trivial things. "You're more agitated than Clelia," I told him.

"Oh, Clelia's already resigned to it," retorted Doro. "It makes me angry, how resigned she is."

"Didn't you expect it?"

"It's like playing the lottery," Doro said. "You put the ticket in your pocket and then you don't think about it."

That afternoon, when Guido stopped the car at the gate, I was with Clelia to say goodbye. I watched her go through the rooms, packing, while the maid ran up and down. Every now and then Clelia would sigh and come to the window where I was leaning, like a hostess making the rounds of her guests, reserving her out-pourings of tiredness and boredom for one of them.

"Are you glad to be going back to Genoa?" I asked. She nodded with a distracted smile.

"Doro likes unexpected trips," I said. "Let's hope this is the last one."

Clelia didn't get this insinuation either. Instead, she said that you can never say never in these matters; then she blushed and wriggled out of it by exclaiming, "Oh, you're horrible!"

I told her I would be leaving the seaside too. I was going home. "I'm sorry," said Clelia. On the contrary, I replied, I was glad to have been with her in her last summer as a girl. For a moment, Clelia reverted to her old self: she paused with her head held high and said softly, "It's true. What a fool I've been! You must have been very bored, poor thing."

They left in the middle of the afternoon, with Guido joking around, but as Clelia immediately showed her lack of enthusiasm, I imagine he stopped. They told me to wait for them, because they expected to be back in a few days; I watched them leave with a certain sadness. Deep down, I was disappointed that Doro hadn't asked me to join them.

The next morning, I was on the beach with Ginetta, and after talking a little about Clelia, I didn't know what else to say when some young men came and took her away. I wandered among the beach umbrellas. I caught a glimpse of Nina and turned away towards the sea. I was expecting Berti to appear at any moment.

Instead, as I walked back down the avenue, I ran into Guido. He had just taken the car to the garage. He told me that the two of them were staying in Genoa. Their doctor was away, and Clelia was feeling a little unwell from the journey. "It's annoying," he said, "everyone's running away this year."

Berti turned up at the trattoria as usual. He entered like a shadow, and I knew he was at my table even before I raised my eyes. He seemed calm.

From his listless and annoyed expression, I would have guessed that he knew about the departure. Instead, he asked me if I had been to the beach that morning. We exchanged a few words, and as we talked, I tried to figure out what I should tell him. I asked him when he was going back to the city.

He made a gesture of annoyance.

"Everyone's going back," I said.

When he heard about Clelia, he fiddled with his matchbox. I hadn't told him the reason for the departure. He seemed mortified, and the thought crossed my mind that he might consider himself the cause because of the incident in the dance hall, so I told him that she had played the good wife, as he wished, and had conceived a child. Berti looked at me without smiling; then he smiled for no apparent reason, put down the matchbox and stammered, "I expected it."

"It's annoying," I said, "that these things happen. Women like Clelia should never fall for it."

Without me noticing the transition, Berti became inconsolable. I remember that as we walked home together, I was silent, and he was silent, his eyes wandering.

"Are you going back to Turin?" I said.

But he wanted to go to Genoa. He asked me to lend him the money for the trip. I told him he was mad. He replied that he could have lied and asked for money to pay off a debt, but that honesty was wasted on me. He just wanted to see Clelia again and say goodbye.

"What do you think?" I exclaimed, "That she remembers you?"

Then he fell silent again. I thought about the strangeness of it all: I had the money for the trip, but I wasn't going. Meanwhile, we reached our alley, and the sight of the olive tree irritated me. I began to understand that nowhere is more uninhabitable than a place where you have been happy. I understood why Doro had taken the train one fine day to return to the hills, only to return to his destiny the next morning.

That evening, we met at the café — everyone was there, including Guido and Nina at her table — and I persuaded Berti to go back to Turin with me. Guido wanted to take us dancing, he was ready to take Berti too. But we left that very night.